King Rupert and the Royal Radishes

A Lesson in Forgiveness and Sharing

by Diane Newsom

illustrated by Terry Knighten

urbanpress

Once upon a time there was a kind king named Rupert who loved radishes.

He loved them so much that he ate them for breakfast, lunch, and dinner every day.

One morning the king sat down to eat his breakfast, and saw that there were no radishes!

He called in his chef and asked, "Why are there no radishes with my breakfast?"

The chef replied, "When I went out to the royal garden this morning to pick some radishes, they were all gone.

Someone must have stolen them!" King Rupert told the chef, "Go to the store and buy some radishes so I can have them for lunch."

When the chef got to the store, they didn't have any radishes either. He asked the store clerk, "Why don't you have any radishes?"

The clerk said, "Someone broke into our store last night and stole all our radishes."

radishes
$1⁵⁰

carrots
$2⁰⁰

The chef went back to the palace and told King Rupert, "No one has any radishes because they were all stolen."

The king told the chef, "Plant more radishes in the garden and have a soldier watch over them so no one steals them, too."

The night before
the radishes were
ready to be picked,
it rained and made
the garden very muddy.

The soldier who was
supposed to guard the
radishes fell asleep
to the gentle pitter
patter of the rain. When
he awakened, all the
radishes were gone!

There were muddy footprints leading away from the garden. The soldier followed the footprints all the way to a house on the edge of a meadow.

The soldier knocked on the door, and a fox opened the door.

The soldier asked, "Do you know anything about the missing radishes?"

The fox said, "The radishes are mine now and I'm keeping them!" The fox quickly closed and locked the door.

The soldier returned to the palace and told the king what had happened. That made King Rupert unhappy and he wanted his radishes back. So he had his soldiers build a giant radish, which had one of his soldiers hiding inside.

They then put the giant radish out in the garden. Sure enough, that night the fox snuck into the garden, grabbed the giant radish and took it to his house.

Once the radish was inside the fox's house, the soldier snuck out of the radish and captured the fox and brought him to King Rupert.

King Rupert asked the fox, "Why did you steal everyone's radishes?"

The fox began to cry and said, "I'm very sorry for taking everyone's radishes. You see, I love radishes, and I like to cook and eat them for every meal. I didn't want to run out of radishes, so I took all the radishes I could find."

King Rupert explained to the fox, "You shouldn't be taking other people's things. You see I also love radishes and eat them with every meal." The king had compassion on the fox and decided to make a deal with him. The king told the fox, "I will let you work with my chef in the palace kitchen to pay for the radishes you have stolen. Part of your pay will be to eat some of the radishes along with me."

King Rupert then said, "You can sit and eat radishes with me every day. When we share the radishes, we can both enjoy eating them."

The fox agreed and they enjoyed eating radishes at every meal while the fox paid the king back for what he had taken.

So remember,
it is wrong to take
anything that doesn't
belong to you.
If you do something
wrong it is always
important for you to
try to make it right.
When you forgive
and share,
you bring joy to
everyone –
including yourself!

FROM THE AUTHOR

This book is dedicated to my brother Scott, who inspired me to create this story for him when he was little. And also to my children, Jessica & Jason, and grandson, Ronan, who helped me keep the story alive. A big thanks to my husband, Jim, who encouraged me to write this, and who is such a great help mate.
I love you all!

ABOUT THE AUTHOR

Diane Newsom is now retired, and enjoys watching her grandson, Ronan during the week. This is her first book, but hopefully not her last. She enjoys sewing, gardening, baking and crafts. She lives in Jeffersonville Indiana with her husband Jim and three dogs.

ABOUT THE ILLUSTRATOR

Dr. Terry Knighten is an award-winning artist who has been creating since childhood. His art ranges from portraits in oil to large scale murals for public art projects. He lives with his wife Michelle in St. Petersburg, Florida.

King Rupert and the Royal Radishes

by Diane Newsom

ISBN 978-1-63360-180-2
For Worldwide Distribution
Printed in the U.S.A.

Urban Press
P.O. Box 8881
Pittsburgh, PA 15221-0881
412.646.2780